Have you read
Book 1 yet?
It was **awful.**

WARNING

This book is
NOT FOR ADULTS.

It is for **YOU.**

If you catch an adult
*(like a parent or
teacher or librarian)*
reading it, or even
touching it, they must
IMMEDIATELY
pay $1 to the nearest
child present.

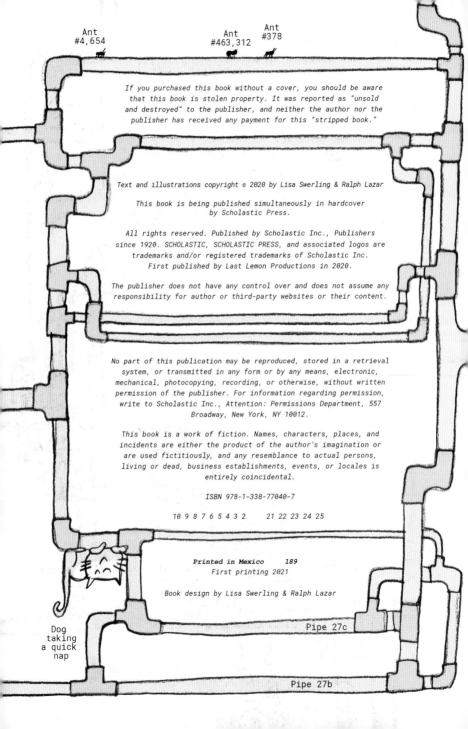

Ant
#4,654

Ant
#463,312

Ant
#378

Text and illustrations copyright © 2020 by Lisa Swerling & Ralph Lazar

This book is being published simultaneously in hardcover
by Scholastic Press.

ISBN 978-1-338-77040-7

10 9 8 7 6 5 4 3 2   21 22 23 24 25

Printed in Mexico   189
First printing 2021

Book design by Lisa Swerling & Ralph Lazar

Dog
taking
a quick
nap

Pipe 27c

Pipe 27b

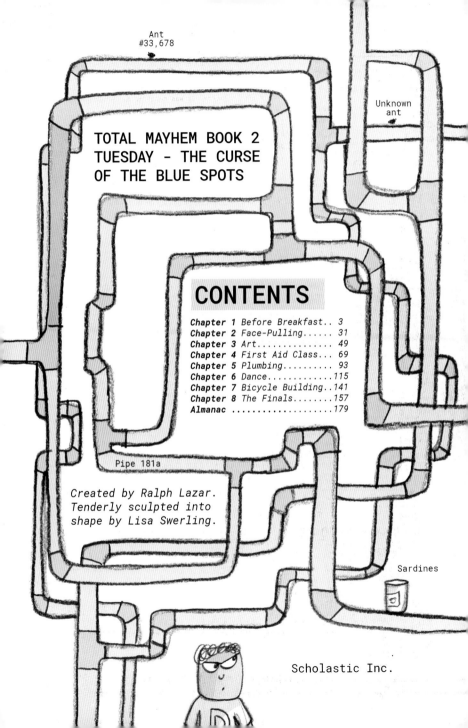

Ant
#33,678

Unknown
ant

**TOTAL MAYHEM BOOK 2
TUESDAY - THE CURSE
OF THE BLUE SPOTS**

CONTENTS

Chapter 1 Before Breakfast.. 3
Chapter 2 Face-Pulling...... 31
Chapter 3 Art.............. 49
Chapter 4 First Aid Class... 69
Chapter 5 Plumbing.......... 93
Chapter 6 Dance............115
Chapter 7 Bicycle Building..141
Chapter 8 The Finals.......157
Almanac 179

Pipe 181a

*Created by Ralph Lazar.
Tenderly sculpted into
shape by Lisa Swerling.*

Sardines

Scholastic Inc.

Things you need to know
before you start
reading this book:

USE THE ALMANAC

There's tons of new info in this book.
If you see something *underlined*
in the story and you don't know
what it is, it'll be in the
Almanac, which is at the
back of the book.

Or online at
total-mayhem.com

BEWARE OF SCALLYWAGS

Scallywags can suddenly pop out
of nowhere. This means you
constantly need to be prepared
for **Total Mayhem Situations.**
Keep your eyes open, stay fit,
and, most importantly, have a
good breakfast. It's the **most
important** meal of the day.
Just ask Dash.

ALWAYS HAVE AT LEAST TWO JOKES AT YOUR DISPOSAL

You never know when you might need to make someone laugh in order to get out of a sticky situation. So always have at least two jokes ready to go If you don't know any right now, how about these?*

[1] What kind of tea is hard to swallow?

[2] How do bees get to school?

*Answers on page 178.

PRACTICE FACE-PULLING

Being able to pull funny/weird/ scary faces can be useful in many ways, something you'll understand by the end of the book. It's worth keeping up to speed on your favorite three or four faces. Practice daily for at least five minutes.

TRY TO LEARN ONE NEW THING EVERY DAY

Today it can be the Figure-8 knot.

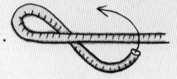

[1] Make a loop with one end.

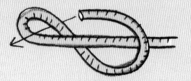

[2] Pass the end through the loop.

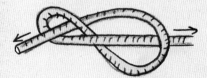

[3] Pull both sides to tighten it.

[4] The finished knot looks like an 8.

ASK FOR TREATS

Even if you've already had
a treat today, no harm in
politely requesting another.

If the adult you're asking
says no, tell them the
youth-of-today
(that includes you)
are the **future**, and it's
important to keep the
youth-of-today well fed.

OKAY, THAT'S IT.
ENJOY THE BOOK.

CHARACTERS

TUESDAY-

The Curse of the Blue Spots

Mindreading-Scallywags
Enemy fighters

Snarling Jetpack-Hog
Enemy fighter

Dash Candoo
Hero of these stories

Ms. Woodhouse
Art teacher

Rob Newman
Dash's best friend

Dr. Williams
First Aid teacher

Mrs. Zhonst
Face-Pulling teacher

Mr. Plumtree
Plumbing teacher

Gronville Honkersmith
Classmate

**Shereena
Aska-Lonka**
Classmate

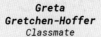

**Greta
Gretchen-Hoffer**
Classmate

Collum Ollum
Classmate

Mrs. Rosebank
*Principal of
Swedhemp
Elementary*

**Professor-
Inspector
Josiah
Stumpnose**
*Principal
of Stumpnose
Elementary*

Mr. Ibis
*Bicycle-Building
teacher*

Mr. Proudfoot
Dance teacher

**Jonjon-Jonjon-
Jonjon Johnson**
*Classmate,
twin of Jeanjean*

**Jeanjean-Jeanjean-
Jeanjean Johnson**
Classmate, twin of Jonjon

Chapter 0

The Giant Exploding Cheesecake

Just kidding!

There is
no giant cheesecake
no explosion
and no
Chapter 0.

Chapter 1

Before Breakfast

It really annoys me
when one gets into a
Total Mayhem Situation
before breakfast.

Which is *exactly* what
happened to me this
morning.

I had just poured
myself a glass of
walrus milk and was
sitting down to my
toasted cabbage
when...

...my **<u>KB-15</u>** started flashing.

In case you didn't already know, a KB-15 is a *Danger Warning Device.*

Danger
was close!

Before I even got to the
front door, they were
inside the house.

Three

Mindreading-
<u>Scallywags</u>

and a _Snarling_ _Jetpack-Hog_.

Mindreading-Scallywags
are a super-dangerous
kind of **scallywag**,
because by reading your
mind,they know what
you're about to do.

This makes fighting them
rather difficult.

Snarling Jetpack-Hogs
don't need much
explaining.

They are hogs, with
jetpacks, that snarl.

They fly fast and are
vicious.

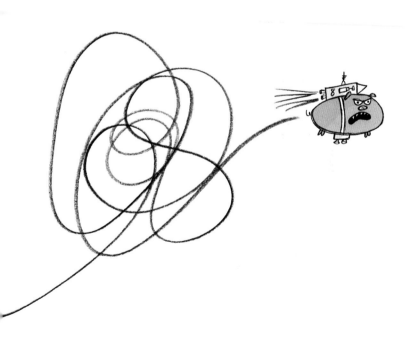

But this being a
Tuesday,
the *worst* day of the
week, I was prepared.

The Mindreading-
Scallywags started
getting into
Mindreading Mode,

which takes
approximately three and
a half seconds to
initiate.

This was **more** than
enough time for me
to pull out my
condensed
expandable
pocket mirror,

and before they could
read my thoughts

it auto-enlarged
and I deployed it.

And not a second too soon.

Their mindreading
beams hit the mirror
and bounced off

back to them,

then back into the
mirror,

and then back to them,

until they were
knocked out.

CRASH! They fell
to the groud!

And, yes, before you
ask, I learned this
trick from the <u>Almanac</u>.

Next was the
Snarling Jetpack-Hog.

It was now in *full
attack mode.*

I sprinted for
the kitchen and it
followed.

I grabbed my glass
of walrus milk,

did a *backflip* over
the Jetpack-Hog,

and then **hurled** the
walrus milk into the
jetpack, instantly
disabling it.

Out of control,
the Jetpack-Hog flew
through the kitchen
window

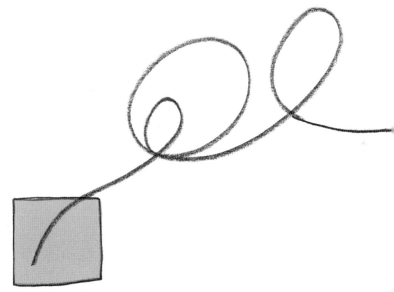

and crashed into the
roof of Mrs. Billysnigg
(the lady who lives
opposite us). Then ran
for its life.

Mrs. Billysnigg had
recently redone her roof
tiles and was NOT happy. →

Game over.

I still had to deal
with the Mindreading-
Scallywags. So I took out my
micro-modulated
shrinkulator

and shrunk them.

By shrinking their
brains to TINY too,
I pulverized their
mindreading power!*

*Sorry to overexplain if you'd
already worked that out.

The shrinking process
woke them up.

When they saw how
small they had become,
**they ran away,
squeaking!**

I then went back to
the kitchen and sat
down to breakfast.

Without walrus milk.

So that's how my day started.

And, yes, it was kind of annoying.

Chapter 2

Face-Pulling

After breakfast
I got changed, packed
my bag, and went off
to my school,
<u>Swedhump Elementary</u>,
THE BEST SCHOOL IN
THE WORLD!

On the way, there
were no incidents.

No *mayhem incidents,*
I mean.

And certainly no
**Total Mayhem
Situations.**

The first lesson
of the day was
Face-Pulling with
Mrs. Zhonst.

She won the
**World Face-Pulling
Championship**, which
was held at the
Uzbükkuu Zoo in 1972
(it's true), so she
commands a lot of
respect in the school,
and our whole general
area.

This lesson was especially important since today was the finals of the **County Inter-School Face-Pulling Championship.**

The two schools in the final were *Swedhump Elementary* (our school) and _Stumpnose Elementary_ (our rival school).

The finals were at the
end of the school day,
and this was our *last
practice*, so we were
all taking it
VERY seriously.

Our top competitors
were Rob Newman
(my best friend) and
Greta Gretchen-Hoffer
(she's *amazing*).

Rob's speciality was the

FGDT

(Full Grimace with Double-Twitch).

Greta's was the

VJDWER
*(Vibrating Jaw-Drop
with Eye-Roll).*

Our sub-champions were:

Collum Ollum with his

PTT

*(Petrified
Triple-Twitch),*

Shereena
Aska-Lonka
with her

PRSF
*(Preposterous
Resting Sour-Face),*

and Gronville Honkersmith's
DSOD
(Dripping Stare of Death).*

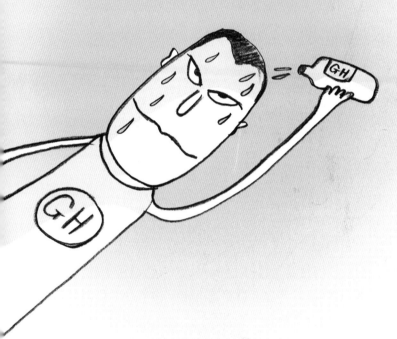

*Gronville likes to pour water from
his water bottle (which he takes
with him *everywhere*) over his face
before doing the **DSOD**, which I have
to admit made it look much scarier.

After the first
practice session,
everyone was quite hot
and tired, so Mrs.
Zhonst said we could
go get a drink at the
water fountain.

Our school has an *epic* water fountain, designed by the great Slovoslochuckian water fountain designer

Andri Grimminik,

whose cousin's son's friend's sister's uncle's aunt's friend's neighbor's dad's brother's friend's daughter's daughter's daughter's daughter's *daughter* had attended our school several years ago.

While we were there,
I noticed that everyone
was drinking water from
the fountain *except
Gronville Honkersmith.*

Instead, he was
drinking from his own
water bottle.

Strange fellow.

We then had another
practice session.

Rob and Greta were
in top form, and
the class ended with us
all feeling **confident**
for the championship
later in the day.

Chapter 3

Art

Next up was art class,
which was in Building F.

Our teacher is
Ms. Woodhouse.

She's really nice and
incredibly talented.

And she's probably
one of the world's
most respected
jump-splodge painters.

In fact, if it were to
be in the Olympics,
I bet you she'd win
the gold medal.

Jump-splodge painting involves jumping off a cupboard (or similar) onto a carefully placed paint tube, which then shoots the paint onto a canvas or wall.

You should try it at home. Parents *love* it.

Ms. Woodhouse can paint
a perfect **anything** by
jump-splodging.

For example, this is
a painting of an
exploding watermelon
that she recently did.*

Don't you just *love* it?

*It was actually bought by
the Sniffsonian
(a very famous museum).

Anyway, today's lesson was **portraits,** so we were divided into pairs to paint each other.

Gronville Honkersmith and Rob were paired up, which was not a good start.

* urk *

Greta and I had to paint
each other. Excellent!

Jonjon-Jonjon-Jonjon
Johnson and his twin
sister, Jeanjean-Jeanjean-
Jeanjean Johnson, were
together (which they did
not look too happy about).

The class began.
Greta kept pulling faces
(hard to paint!), but I
didn't mind since, as far
as I was concerned, the
more practice she got
before the final, the
better!

Jonjon-Jonjon-Jonjon Johnson and *Jeanjean-Jeanjean-Jeanjean Johnson* had a fight, and he threw some paint at her.

She then threw some
paint back at him

and started to cry.

And when *Jeanjean-
Jeanjean-Jeanjean
Johnson* cries, boy,
does she cry.

The tears formed a puddle and *Jonjon-Jonjon-Jonjon Johnson* slipped in it.

Ms. Woodhouse had to have a bit of a chat with them to avoid a **major escalation.**

When things had calmed
down, we continued
with our portraits.

After half an hour of
painting, Ms. Woodhouse
came to inspect our
hard work.

Jonjon-Jonjon-Jonjon
by
Jeanjean-Jeanjean-Jeanjean

Collum
by
Shereena

Shereena
by
Collum

Gronville
by
Rob

Rob
by
Gronville

Jeanjean-Jeanjean-Jeanjean
by
Jonjon-Jonjon-Jonjon

Greta
by
me

Me
by
Greta

Ms. Woodhouse took
one look at them
and started to
frown.

"Why have you all
painted blue spots
on each other's
portraits?"
she demanded.

And then she looked at us, face-to-actual-face, and we looked at each other, and we realized that we were *all* covered in blue spots *in real life.*

The spots *are* actually blue, but because this is a black-and-white book, you can't tell. If you put on your <u>converter-glasses</u>, the book will immediately become **full color**, and then you'll see how blue they actually are.

All of us!
And it wasn't paint!

They were actual spots!

On everyone!

Except
Gronville Honkersmith.

What the heggleswick was going on?

Chapter 4

First Aid Class

Luckily, the next class was *First Aid* with
Dr. Williams.

She has some of the world's most fancy medical equipment.

She also happens to be one of the world's most famous **ant breeders.**

This is Dr. Williams at ant farm 27b, which is in her kitchen.

This is Dr. Williams
at ant farm 41a, which
is in her bedroom.

Ant farm 41a has been rated a *Highly Prestigious Farm*. It is extremely competitive to get in, and most ants spend at least two years preparing for the admissions interview to get a place on the farm.

Some of her ants are trained to operate the fancy medical equipment.

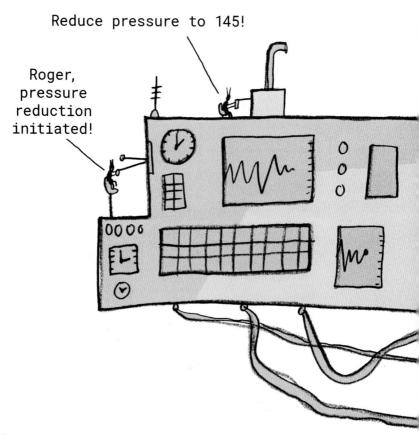

Reduce pressure to 145!

Roger, pressure reduction initiated!

Dr. Williams
inspected our blue
spots closely.

Her findings:

① Looks weird.
② Will go away
   in a few days.
③ Don't worry.

Her **CMA**
(Chief Medical Ant)
agreed.

I agree!

Phew! What a relief
(that CMA really
knows her stuff).

But then ...

... disaster!

When we tried
face-pulling, the
spots **itched** like
crazy.

This wasn't good!

It would ruin our chances at the competition.

We **REALLY** did not
want to lose to
Stumpnose Elementary.

General aura of
horribleness
(plus a hint of
sardine smell)

Their principal,
**Professor-Inspector
Josiah Stumpnose,**
is a HORRIBLE man, and
if they won the trophy,
he would boast about it
for years to come.

Because everyone was
a little upset, Dr.
Williams recommended
a spot of Wellness.

To help us relax,
she said we could
listen to her famous
ant choir *Prodigiosus
Cantus Formicae** for the
rest of class.

*"The Amazing
Singing Ants"
in Latin.

Halfway through the performance, out of the corner of my eye, I saw Gronville Honkersmith sneaking out of class.

Hmm, suspicious.

I snuck out too and
followed close behind
(but not too close).

He left the building
and headed for the
Science Lab.*

*And don't ask me why it's
shaped like a banana
because I have no idea.

In we went.

What was he doing?

I peered
round the
corner...

...and saw him
standing in front
of a mirror.

Pulling faces!

While the rest of us were itching away, Gronville was mastering **The Art of Face-Pulling** with secret practice!

And he was
getting AMAZING.

Did Gronville have some
big plan to get the
glory for himself?

← You may not
realize it, but
this is a highly
advanced
face-pull.

Still worried,
I returned to First
Aid class, where the
ants were just
finishing off the
most beautiful song.

Dr. Williams was
so proud.

Everyone cheered and
class was over.

Chapter 5

Plumbing

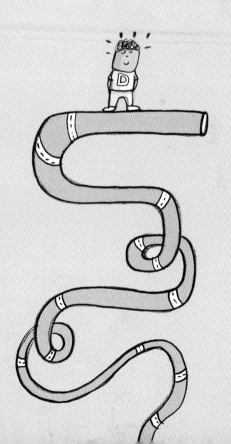

Our next class was
Plumbing with
Mr. Plumtree.

We have no idea how
he got that dent in
his head, so don't
even ask.

I **love** this class because we get to play with pipes and water.

What's *not* to enjoy?

Before Mr. Plumtree got a job at our school, he was the world's most sought-after **Royal Plumber**.

He only worked on *castles* and *mega-mega-mansions* of **kings** and **queens**.

He was so successful that he *didn't even bother* with the castles and mansions of mere princes and princesses.

He plumbed the showers of
the **Royal Palace of
Middle-Ostentia.**

He plumbed
the swimming
pool of
**King Edmond
the Gurkk.**

This is just a
small section of
the castle. It
has over 700
rooms in total.

PERCIVAL
PLUMTREE
ROYAL
PLUMBING
SERVICES

He plumbed the hot tub
of **Queen Jezebel** of
**South-Northern
Swottolia.**

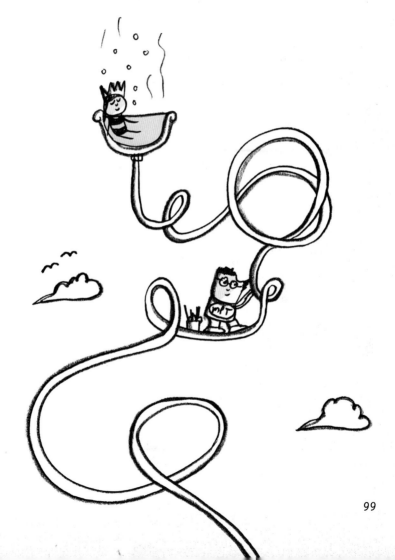

And he plumbed the waterslide of **King Boris McBoris-Boris-Swad-Widge.**

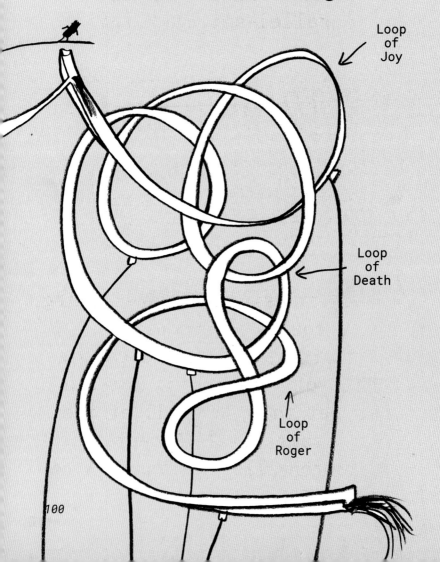

Loop
of
Joy

Loop
of
Death

Loop
of
Roger

Today's lesson was on how to extract triple-nozzles from a **double-nozzle parallel-spigot-valve.**

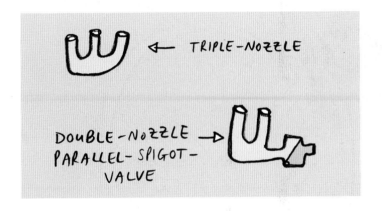

Although it was deeply fascinating, I couldn't concentrate.
I just wasn't able to get my mind off the spots. How did we get them, and all at the same time? (Except Gronville ... hmmm ...)

Think, Dash, *think*.

I did think, and a
sort-of-thought came
and hovered over me,
then came a bit
closer, and then
turned into a **proper,
actual** thought.

The water fountain!
We all drank from the
water fountain — except
Gronville! Of course!

Shortly after that,
the spots came up.

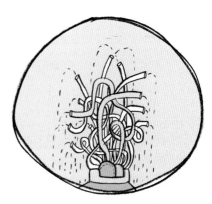

I had to
investigate,
and **quickly.**

I pulled a
freeze-bomb out of
my backpack and
activated it,

which was quite
hilarious since
Mr. Plumtree **froze**
just as he was about
to take a gulp of
water.

I had exactly fifteen
minutes till the freeze-
bomb wore off, so I ran
to the fountain. There
wasn't much to see.

I knew that the water
for the fountain came
from the **pump room**,
which was under
Mr. Plumtree's classroom.

So that's exactly where

I'd never been in a
pump room before, and
I do have to say,
it was GREAT!

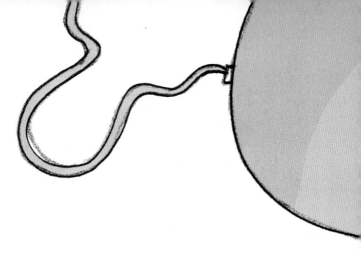

Then I noticed them.
Muddy footprints!

I followed them out the
back door of the pump room
to the flower bed at the
school's outer wall.

The prints ended
(or should I say *started*)
at the wall.
Very suspicious.
Very suspicious indeed.

Someone must have jumped
from the wall into the
flower bed, gone into the
pump room, and then...

...then **what**?
And **who**?
And **why**?

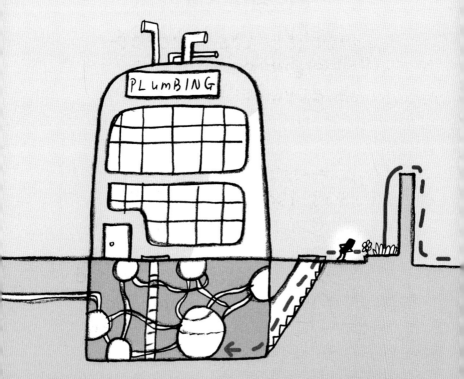

I was running out of
time, so I rushed back
to Mr. Plumtree's class.

Just as the end-of-
lesson bell rang,
everyone unfroze.

The class
roared with
laughter as
water splashed
all over poor
Mr. Plumtree.

And with that,
we headed off
to our next
class.

Chapter 6

Dance

Next up was Dance
class in the
school theater.

Mr. Proudfoot.
is our dance teacher,
and we all **LOVE** him.

He was
World Snow-Dancing
Champion
in *2018*, so the school
is very proud of him.

When Mr. Proudfoot
does his snow dance,
it snows.
it snows.

Always.

And not just any old snow,
but massive blizzards.

When he won the World
Championship, everyone
actually had to be
evacuated from the stadium
on giant rescue sleds.

As a result, he is
forbidden from doing
his snow dance on
school premises.

Today was exciting
for two reasons:

[1] We were learning
the **Flamingo Shuffle**,
which is really fun.

[2] The finals of the County Inter-School Face-Pulling Championship were being held in this very theater, and the **trophy** was already in its place on the stage.

Do NOT laugh at the trophy. It's very beautiful. Really.

The trophy is a solid-
platinum face cast of
Delia Snainsbury, first-
ever winner of the
competition.

She's legendary. She's
112 years old and still
competes, though obviously
not at school level.

Just as we were about to start the dance class, we all noticed a strange smell of sardines. A dark figure appeared ominously at the theater entrance.

It was
**Professor-Inspector
Josiah Stumpnose**
himself. Principal of
Stumpnose Elementary.

He'd come for the final
polishing of the trophy.

As he was polishing it,
I noticed something fishy
(even more fishy than the
smell of sardines):

muddy shoes!

The mysterious pump room visitor!

What was he up to?

When Professor-
Inspector Josiah
Stumpnose left,
everyone was so busy
working on their
Flamingo Shuffles

that I managed to
sneak after him
unnoticed.

I jumped into the luggage
box of his motorbike just
as he was pulling out.

We drove all the way to
Stumpnose Elementary

and parked in his
actual office.

(I have to say, the smell
of sardines was pretty
unbelievable.)

When he left to make some tea, I snuck out for a quick look around.

The first thing I noticed was two books on his desk:

[1] *How to Tame and Train a Snarling Jetpack-Hog*

and

[2] *Mindreading-Scallywag Mayhem Moves.*

So, he was the one who'd sent those troublemakers to my house!

Then I saw a bottle.

Blue Spot Compound.

The stuff looked
1 serious
2 dangerous
3 not good.

Aha!

It was all
suddenly clear!

1 He'd poured some of
the Blue Spot Compound
into a pipe in the
pump room

2 and it had
traveled to the
fountain.

③ We drank from the fountain

④ that gave us the spots

⑤ that itched when we pulled the faces,

⑥ that will make us **lose the finals.**

Pure evil!

Then I saw another
bottle.

It was the **Blue Spot
Antidote.**

Or, should I say,
the ANTI-DOT!

Just what we
needed to get rid
of the spots!

As I pocketed the two bottles, I heard a sound behind me.

He was there at the door.

"Dash Candoo,
you think you know
everything!"
he shouted.

**"But now you are
my prisoner!"**

He pulled a lever
and a net dropped
from the ceiling.

"See you later,"
he sneered.
"I'll release you
after **we've won
the trophy!**"

And with that, he reversed
his motorbike out of his
office,triple-bolted the
door, and was off.

I was *well and truly*
trapped.

Chapter 7

Bicycle Building

This is a
quadcycle
(a four-wheeler).

The next lesson of
the day was
Bicycle Building
with Mr. Ibis.

Before he came to teach
at our school, Mr. Ibis
was **world famous** for
having won the
Tour de *South-Northern
Swottolia* on a noncycle*
he built while
blindfolded.

*Look up under <u>Loma-99</u> in
the Almanac.

That bicycle, the Loma-99, was on display in our school museum, and everyone was very proud of it.

It is actually said to be worth over **forty million** dollars.

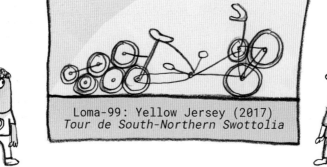

Loma-99: Yellow Jersey (2017)
Tour de South-Northern Swottolia

It's also rumored that Mr. Ibis used to work at **Darwin Cycles**, the TOP-SECRET **quadcycle** factory, and that he was instrumental in the development of early backpack-release models.

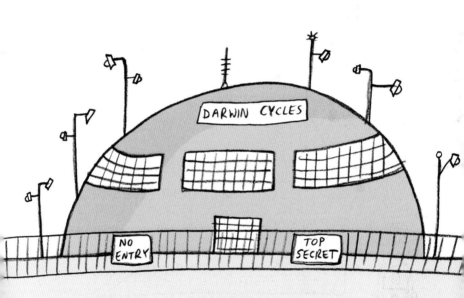

Anyway, in today's
lesson we were
finishing off our
tandem bikes.

Or we were *meant*
to be.

When Rob noticed my
absence, he knew
something serious was up,
since I'd never miss a
Bicycle-Building class.

He opened up his
TTD (_Transponder_
Tracking Device) to
see if he could pick
up a signal from me.

Rob and I carry concealed TTDs at all times. This lets us locate each other in **emergencies**.

And this was an emergency!

Rob immediately picked up my precise location.

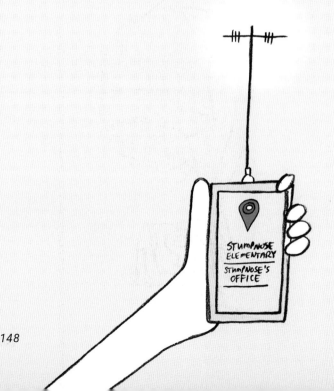

He decided to deploy his
warp-vortex.

He said the password
(which I can't tell you)
and ...

...in a
flash he was
sucked up.

Half a micro-
nanosecond later,
he was with me.

At first, Rob laughed
to see me trapped
like this.

"Very unlike you,
Dash!" he chuckled.

Despite the fact
that he had an
MRX-34 Laser on him,
it took quite a long
time to cut me free.

As soon as I was out, we said the password again, and in a flash we were sucked into the warp-vortex.

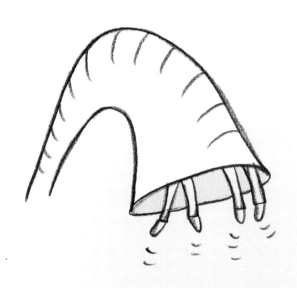

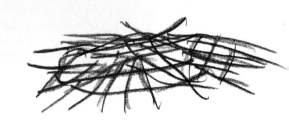

A trilli-second later,
we were back in
Mr. Ibis's class.

Nobody had even
noticed we were gone.

The Johnson twins were arguing (as usual).

Rob and I each took a sip of the antidote

and within seconds
the blue spots had
disappeared!

Then an announcement came over the school **snintercom**.*

"All students please proceed to the theater. The Face-Pulling Championship is about to commence."

*A snintercom is like a nintercom ... I mean ... an intercom, but better.

Chapter 8

The Finals

As our team lined up,
I passed them the
antidote.

Everyone took a sip and
their spots *immediately*
disappeared.

The judges of the competition were professionals brought in from the IFA *(International Face-Pulling Association)*.

They sat up on the stage and looked quite scary.

While we were waiting for the two principals to arrive, I snuck behind Professor-Inspector Stumpnose's chair, poured a few drops of the compound into his teacup, and then took my position with the rest of our team.

As *(horrible)* Team Stumpnose arrived, the professor-inspector looked at us in surprise.

We could tell he didn't know *what* was going on.

Where were our spots?

And when he saw **ME**, he turned sort of *greenish*.*

*His skin color in real life is greenish. Again, you can't quite tell because this is a *black-and-white* book.

If you put on your converter-glasses, the book will immediately become **full color** and you'll see what I mean.

To calm his nerves, he took a **big** sip of tea.

Through his already green face, I could see small blue spots starting to form.

Our team donned their capes, the commencement trumpet sounded, and the finals began.

Stumpnose Elementary
didn't stand a chance.

Rob's *Full Grimace*
with Double-Twitch
was **EPIC.**

Collum Ollum's *Petrified Triple-Twitch* was PETRIFYING.

Greta's *Vibrating Jaw-Drop with Eye-Roll* was **LEGENDARY.**

Shereena Aska-Lonka's *Preposterous Resting Sour-Face* was **truly PREPOSTEROUS.**

And I have to admit,
Gronville Honkersmith
CRUSHED IT with his
Dripping Stare of Death.

When Stumpnose realized that his team was being **PULVERIZED**, he began to huff and snort like an enraged hippopotamus.

This of course made his face itch like crazy.
The more he itched, the more faces he pulled. And the more faces he pulled, the itchier he got.

RESULT!

We won by *seventeen points*, a **record** for a final.

Mrs. Zhonst went totally *berserk*.

She said this was a bigger deal than her winning the **World Face-Pulling Championship** at the *Uzbükkuu Zoo* in 1972!

As we raised the trophy and cheered, out of the corner of my eye I saw ...

...Professor-Inspector
Stumpnose storming out
of the hall in a
VERY MAJOR (and spotty)
huff, followed by his
horrible team.

What a day!

- The End -

Answers to jokes from page 5:
[1] Reality [2] On the buzz.

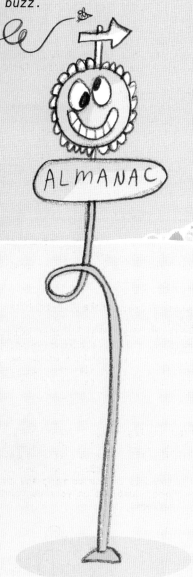

Almanac

The COMPLETE ALMANAC is the place where you can find out everything about Dash and his world.

It's online at total-mayhem.com/almanac. This is the Book 2 Almanac, providing detailed information for Total Mayhem Book 2.

Andri Grimminik

Andri Grimminik Herr-Groggen-Chommen-Hummen-Grekken is arguably the world's most famous water fountain designer. He was born in Slovoslochuckia and makes fountains for the rich and famous worldwide. His cousin's son's friend's sister's uncle's aunt's friend's neighbor's dad's brother's friend's daughter's daughter's daughter's daughter's daughter attended Swedhump Elementary.

Famous clients of his include:
- King Edmond the Gurkk
- Queen Jezebel of South-Northern Swottolia
- The Bog-Slotnigg Water Park
- President William Williamson of Williamsville

Condensed Expandable Pocket Mirror (CEPM)

Small, concealable mirror that expands on deployment. Can be used to repel enemy beams (like mindreading beams or melt-beams). Can also be used for communication, for starting fires, and as an actual mirror.

Converter-Glasses

Converter-glasses make things look the way they should be. For instance, if you've got a black-and-white photo but want to see it in full color, just put on your converter-glasses. If you wake up in the morning and look awful in the mirror, same thing: Just put on your converter-glasses and you'll look amazing!

Flamingo Shuffle

The Flamingo Shuffle is a world-famous dance created and choreographed by Mr. Proudfoot. In it, dancers mimic flamingos. It's so effective that if done in areas where flamingos live, they might well come and join in. There was a famous incident in 2017 when a live performance at the school was unwisely held during the annual flamingo migration, and over one million birds descended on Swedhump Elementary. The show had to be canceled and the school was closed for a week, as special cleaners needed to come in to get rid of all the droppings. Can you imagine, a million flamingo poos!

Freeze-Bombs

As the name suggests, these weapons freeze every-thing within fifty yards of the explosion. The effect lasts exactly fifteen minutes.

They can be really fun if you time them well. A freeze-bomb explodes two seconds after it's been thrown. If you time it just as someone is pouring a glass of water or about to jump into a pool, when the freeze effect wears off, it can be really funny.

Jump-Splodge Painting

Highly sophisticated and respected art form. Jump-splodge painting involves jumping off a cupboard onto carefully placed paint tubes, which then shoot the paint onto a canvas or wall.

Ms. Woodhouse is probably one of the world's most respected jump-splodge painters.

KB-15

Imminent Danger Warning Device (IDWD)
KB-15 Flash Codes:
* Red — on-off 1-second intervals continuous: Imminent Danger.
* Red — on 2s, off 2s: Imminent lightning storm.
* Green — on 3s, off 1s: Takeout delivery almost here.
* Blue — on 5s, off 5s: Battery needs charging.

Loma-99

Extraordinary noncycle on which Mr.
Ibis won the Tour de South-Northern
Swottolia (a legendary mountain-biking
race). He built it while blindfolded.
It's in the museum at Swedhump
Elementary.

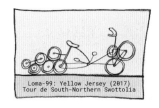

Loma-99: Yellow Jersey (2017)
Tour de South-Northern Swottolia

Micro-Modulated Shrinkulator

Highly sophisticated device that shrinks things.
Only to be used if you have a Clearance
Certificate, which requires three months of
training. Once you shrink something with it, it
cannot be undone. REPEAT, it CANNOT be undone.

Mindreading-Scallywags

How common: Moderately
Special power: Mindreading, mind-bending
Weakness: Scared of mirrors
Typical group size: 3 or more
Operate alone? Hardly ever
Maximum jump distance: 8 feet
Cleverness: 7/10
Speed: 4/10
Agility: 4/10

MRX-34 Laser

Small, concealable, very powerful laser.
Ideal for cutting through things.
Can also be used for communication.

Prodigiosus Cantus Formicae Ant Choir

This is the world's most famous ant choir.
Trained and taught by Dr. Williams.
They also have a dance routine,
choreographed by Mr. Proudfoot.
"Prodigiosus Cantus Formicae" is Latin
for "The Amazing Singing Ants."

Quadcycles

Four-wheeled cycles that can fold up into a
backpack and be deployed by mind activation.
The wheel configuration constantly adapts
to the terrain and is controlled by a very
sophisticated sensor (or "brain") embedded in
the saddle. A quadcycle looks easy to ride,
but it is actually quite difficult.

A three-week introductory course at the QTA (Quadcycle Training Academy) is highly recommended.

Quadcycle Maintenance:
Pretty much the same as regular bicycle maintenance, apart from the sneggle-sprocket. Keep the drive chain clean and well lubricated, make sure brake-fluid pressure is good, check all nuts and bolts before and after big missions, make sure the tires are in good condition, and finally, and most importantly, make sure the sneggle-sprocket is smooth and has enough lemon juice on it at all times. Make sure the lemon juice compression canister is fully primed to at least level eight, especially before big missions.

Scallywags
There are many different types of scallywag. Each type has its own fighting techniques, strengths, and weaknesses.

Snarling Jetpack-Hogs
Snarling Jetpack-Hogs don't need much explanation. They are hogs, with jetpacks, that snarl. Often accompany Mindreading-Scallywags. They fly fast and are vicious. Allergic to walrus milk.

Snintercom
A snintercom is an advanced wireless intercom that also has DTC (Document Transfer Capacity). Its base portal is in Mrs. Rosebank's office, from where she can make verbal announcements to the whole school. But it is mainly used to send paper memos or piles of documents or even books to everyone in the school. Likewise they can send documents to her via snintercom. The maximum capacity for a single send is seven books. Collum Ollum, for fun, once tried to send the Complete & Comprehensive Encyclopedia of Grobsnots (21 volumes), and he jammed the system. It took technicians a week to repair and the encyclopedia was lost forever. He got into a lot of trouble for it.

Stumpnose Elementary

Principal: Professor Inspector Josiah Stumpnose.
Rival school to Swedhump Elementary.
Smells of sardines in some areas.
Most kids who attend this school are known to be:
[1] awful or
[2] rude or
[3] mean or
[4] have terrible table manners or
[5] all of the above.

Swedhump Elementary

Dash's school.
Principal: Mrs. Rosebank.
Probably the best school in the world.
Definitely has the best teachers in the world.
Named after the hump of a swed, a two-faced humped creature.

Transponder Tracking Device (TTD)

Dash and Rob always carry micro-versions of these.
They allow them to find each other in emergencies —
provided the device has been activated.
So, for example, if Rob gets captured but is unable
to activate his TTD, he won't send a signal.

Walrus Milk

It's quite dangerous milking a walrus. But worth it, because
their milk is delicious. Dash has a distant relative who is
friendly with the brother of a man whose best friend's sister's
uncle's aunt's son's son has a walrus farm, and so Dash is
able to get supplies.

Warp-Vortex
A warp-vortex allows the warpee (owner) plus sub-warpee (passenger) to move from one place to another in a trilli-second. Warp-vortexes are typically backpack-mounted. Pocket versions exist but are quite expensive.

Each warp-vortex has its own password, which the users will not share under any circumstances (so don't even ask).

World Face-Pulling Championship
The WFPC is an annual event held at the Uzbükkuu Zoo that attracts the world's top face-pullers, not only because of the prestige, but also because of the prize money.

1st prize: $12,000,000
2nd prize: $5,000,000
3rd prize: $12.75

List of some WFPC winners this century:
2000: Rodney the Ossifier
2001: Rodney the Ossifier
2002: Maureen Zhonst
2003: Shaila & Adan Gómez (tied 1st place)
2004: Canceled due to a grobsnot infestation
2005: Ben & Eileen Dover (tied 1st place)
2006: Canceled due to invizizz migration
2007: Humperdinck Swedgewidge-Holstein
2008: Wolraad Woltemaade
2009: Jezebela the Marauder
2010: Genevieve the Ossifier (cousin of Rodney the Ossifier)
2011: Humperdinck Swedgewidge-Holstein
2012: Lara Leigh McFabulous
2013: Siena Rennie
2014: Mika Haberling
2015: Gabriel Tarrow
2016: Heeza Nidyitt
2017: Ima Nidyitt (twin sister of Heeza)
2018: Maxwellian Wald
2019: Julian & Lukas Jammy (tied 1st place)
2020: Jamie el-Nagapie

This is the end of this book's Almanac.
For the **complete Almanac***, go to:*

www.total-mayhem.com

HERE'S A VERY
SNEAKY PEEK AT

It REALLY annoys me when
one gets into a
Total Mayhem Situation
before breakfast.

Which is exactly what
happened to me this
morning.

I had just poured
myself a glass of
<u>osteop milk</u>...

and was sitting down
to warm slice of
<u>pizzup</u>.

I was just thinking how
pizzup is my **absolutely
favorite food...**

...when my <u>KB-15</u>
started flashing **red.**

Danger was close!
I didn't even have
time to prepare.

I went straight to the
front door.

Opened it...

...nothing.

How strange.

KB-15s are normally **100%** accurate.

In fact, all KB-15s come with a *Lifetime Warranty.* There are no documented examples of KB-15s failing in **any** situations **ever**, unless of course the batteries have not been charged. I make sure mine are **always** fully charge. You should too. And if you don't have a KB-15, you should get one. Really.

Then I heard a rustle in the <u>smellephant grass</u>

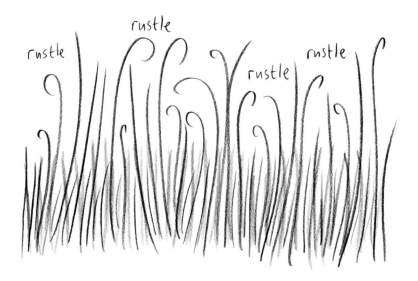

Smellephant grass grows wild where I live. And I guess you know why it's called that, right? Because <u>smellephants</u> **LOVE** it.

And there they were.
Suddenly.

Five
<u>Forest-Scallywags</u>!

This was not good.

Forest-Scallywags are
MASTERS of camouflage.

They immediately began
to attack using
Move #18,854
The Rolling Starfish*.

STEP 1: Launch

STEP 2: Inversion

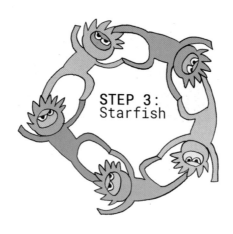

STEP 3:
Starfish

*This is a HIGHLY dangerous and very technical move. **DO NOT** try this at home without consulting the Almanac.

FOR DASH CANDOO, EVERY DAY IS . . .

TOTAL MAYHEM!

TOTAL MAYHEM 1
MONDAY INTO THE CAVE OF THIEVES
RALPH LAZAR
SCHOLASTIC

TOTAL MAYHEM 2
TUESDAY THE CURSE OF THE BLUE SPOTS
RALPH LAZAR
SCHOLASTIC

TOTAL MAYHEM 3
WEDNESDAY THE FOREST OF SECRETS
RALPH LAZAR
SCHOLASTIC

ABOUT THE CREATORS

Ralph Lazar and Lisa Swerling live in California.

Ralph made up the Dash stories (inspired by wrestling his godson — Dash!) and did the drawings. Lisa shaped the stories into this book.

Ralph and Lisa are New York Times *bestselling authors, and the creators of the popular illustrated project* Happiness Is..., *which has been translated into over twenty languages and has over three million followers online.*